What is a Novel?

Charlotte Guillain

raintree

a Capstone company — publishers for children

Raintree is an imprint of Capstone Global Library Limited, a company incorporated in England and Wales having its registered office at 7 Pilgrim Street, London, EC4V 6LB – Registered company number: 6695582

www.raintree.co.uk
myorders@raintree.co.uk

Edited by Clare Lewis and Holly Beaumont
Designed by Philippa Jenkins
Picture research by Wanda Winch
Originated by Capstone Global Library Ltd
Produced by Helen McCreath
Printed and Bound in China by CTPS

ISBN 978 1 406 29002 8
18 17 16 15 14
10 9 8 7 6 5 4 3 2 1

British Library Cataloguing in Publication Data
A full catalogue record for this book is available from the British Library.

Acknowledgements
We would like to thank the following for permission to reproduce photographs: Alamy: Matthew Taylor, 16, Network Photographers, 10, Photostock-Israel/Chad Shahar, 24, Steven May, 17; Capstone: Josh Alves, 9, Capstone Studio: Karon Dubke, 13; Getty Images Inc: Neilson Barnard, 25, The Image Bank/ Cavan Images, 5; iStockphoto: Duncan 1890, 14; Newscom: picture-alliance/DPA/Jens Buettner, 12, picture-alliance/DPA/Oliver Berg, 11, Polaris/Stephanie Keith, 8, Zuma Press/Ian Gavan, 18; Rex USA: Geoffrey Swaine, 21, Rex, 15, Rex/Heathcliff O'Malley, 22; Shutterstock: Angela Harburn, 20, Dmitry Morgan, 7, Elena Schweitzer, 19, Jacek Chabraszewski, 23, Michael C. Gray, 4, prudkov, 27, Samuel Borges Photography, 26, sunabesyou, 28, urfin, pencil.

Disclaimer
All the internet addresses (URLs) given in this book were valid at the time of going to press. However, due to the dynamic nature of the internet, some addresses may have changed, or sites may have changed or ceased to exist since publication. While the author and publishers regret any inconvenience this may cause readers, no responsibility for any such changes can be accepted by either the author or the publishers.

Contents

Some words are shown in bold, **like this**. You can find out what they mean by looking in the glossary.

What do you like to read?

Every day we all read so many different things. We read instructions at school and messages from friends. You might read magazines or comics. But one of the most enjoyable things to read is a novel. When we pick up a novel and start to read, we can be taken away on an amazing adventure or discover another world, full of interesting characters.

Reading novels can be a great way to relax.

You can visit a local bookshop to discover new novels.

Do you enjoy reading novels? If you are not that keen, then perhaps you haven't yet found the right one for you. Read on to find out more about the many different types of novels out there, just waiting for you to discover them!

see for yourself

Go to your local library or bookshop and look at the novels on the shelves for your age group. Have a look at the covers of a few books. What do the images on the covers tell you about the stories inside them? Read the **blurb** on the back cover to see if it hooks you in and makes you want to read the book.

What is a novel?

What makes a novel different to other types of writing? You will often find the following features in a novel:

- The story it tells is **fiction**. Even when a story is based on real events, the author of a novel has researched the real-life experience and created something original.

- Novels have a **narrative** told by a storyteller.

- Novels usually have a certain number of pages and are not too short. Because of their length, novels are usually broken up into chapters or sections.

See for yourself

We can read novels in different ways. Most novels are published as physical books that we put on our shelves, but many are also published as e-books. People read these on e-readers or on their phones, tablets or computers. Whichever way we read these books, they are still novels.

You may prefer reading novels on an e-reader or from a book.

- Most novels are written in **prose**. This means the language hasn't been organized or made to rhyme like poetry.

- Novels can be written in different **genres**. For example, some novels are adventure stories, while others can be funny or mysterious.

Characters

When you read a good novel, you feel like you are getting to know the main characters. You may even miss them when you finish reading the story! Real and believable characters are important for a story to work.

Write your own

When you are developing characters for your own stories, start by asking lots of questions about them. What is their name and how old are they? Where do they live and what do they look like? What do they like and dislike? Ask as many questions as you can and get to know your characters as you answer them.

Zeke Meeks is the main character in the *Zeke Meeks vs...* books. Many readers will relate to his love of video games and TV.

In most novels there is usually one main character, or **protagonist**, who is the key person we get to know in the story. This person is often trying to reach a goal and has to overcome problems on the way.

Sometimes there might be two or three protagonists, telling the story from different viewpoints. There will also be other types of characters in the story, for example someone who gets in the way of the protagonist to stop them getting what they want. Other characters will help or support the main character.

Plot

The **plot** is what happens in a story. Novels are longer than other types of story and can have a more complex plot. Often a novel will have one main plot running through the whole book, with shorter sub-plots cropping up at different stages of the story. The main plot will usually revolve around what the main character wants. As this character tries to achieve their goal, their decisions and activities affect what happens in the plot.

Many writers plan the plots of their stories on cards so they can move things around.

Famous fiction

Jeff Kinney, author of *Diary of a Wimpy Kid*, starts his books by thinking of lots of good jokes. He then sees how he can link up the jokes and find a theme to create a plot for a new story. He writes several different drafts of the story, developing and changing the plot each time.

Jeff Kinney is a cartoonist as well as a writer.

In most good stories there will often be a "rug-pulling moment". This happens when the main character is in trouble and it seems impossible for them to get what they want. It is usually followed by the character overcoming his or her problems and moving on. Some stories have a surprising twist at the end to keep readers on their toes!

Voice and tense

The "voice" of a story is important. Some novels are written in the **first person** so, for example, "I walked down the path". The main character narrates the story from his or her viewpoint and it seems as if they are talking directly to us, telling us about their thoughts and feelings. In a first-person story, the reader only knows the narrator's viewpoint.

Hearing an author read their own work is very exciting.

In a **third-person** voice, the author stands back from the characters and describes what they think and do, for example, "Joe walked down the path". The writer can tell us about various different characters' viewpoints so we get more information about what is happening.

Are your favourite novels written in first or third person?

Writers also have to choose which tense to write in. If they write in the **present tense** – "She climbs up the tree" – the story can feel very immediate and exciting. Other stories are written in the **past tense** – "She climbed up the tree".

Write your own

When you have an idea for a story, experiment with the voice and tense before you start writing. How does your storytelling change if you switch from third person to first person? Will your story suit the past tense, or would it be more exciting in the present tense?

Adventure stories

Lots of people love adventure stories. These novels are popular because the characters are taken away from their everyday lives and often have to overcome danger in order to reach their goal. This makes them very exciting!

Adventure stories have been popular for many years and some classic adventure novels are still read a lot today, such as *The Silver Sword* and *Treasure Island*.

Treasure Island is a thrilling adventure story, full of pirates and chests of gold.

Famous fiction

Willard Price wrote exciting adventure stories for children, such as *Volcano Adventure* and *Arctic Adventure*. In these stories, two teenagers called Hal and Roger travel the world, saving animals and surviving danger! In 2011, *Leopard Adventure*, the first of a new series of stories about Hal's son and Roger's daughter, was published. Anthony McGowan is writing the new books, which should appeal to readers who loved the first series.

Anthony McGowan is a prize-winning author of books for children and young adults.

A good adventure story should:

- be completely gripping so that the reader doesn't want to stop turning the pages

- be full of surprises so the reader doesn't know what will happen next

- include strong, brave heroes who are not afraid to take risks, and wonderfully wicked baddies who will stop at nothing to get what they want

- completely take the reader away from reality.

Funny novels

Funny novels are very popular. Most people enjoy laughing and sharing the jokes in a book with their friends. Making readers laugh out loud is very hard for writers to achieve and takes a lot of skill and practice. The funniest writers read a lot of other humorous books, and watch comedy films and television programmes.

Cressida Cowell has sold millions of copies of her entertaining stories.

Famous fiction

The *Mr Gum* books by Andy Stanton are famously funny, but they don't follow all the rules we expect with a novel. The plots of the stories are often completely crazy and Andy plays around with language in completely original and unexpected ways.However, he still includes characters the reader cares about, as well as deliciously horrible villains.

Andy's author events are as funny as his books!

The funniest novels have the following features:

- They are original. Writers won't make their readers laugh if they've heard all the jokes and twists before.

- They play around with words in surprising ways. When writers play with the different possible meanings of a word it is called a **pun**.

- Most funny stories still need to have a strong **plot** that makes sense and believable characters.

Fantasy novels

If you want to escape from ordinary life for a while, then a fantasy novel is perfect. Fantasy stories take the reader to new worlds that can be filled with magical creatures and powerful heroes and villains. *Harry Potter*, *The Hobbit*, *The Worst Witch* and the *Artemis Fowl* novels are all well-known fantasy books.

Famous fiction

J.K. Rowling's *Harry Potter* books are among the best-known children's fantasy novels in the world. Harry is a young wizard who goes to Hogwarts School of Witchcraft and Wizardry and gets involved in exciting and dangerous adventures. Around 450 million copies of the seven books in the series have been sold and they have been translated into 67 languages.

J.K. Rowling is one of the most famous authors in the world.

In many fantasy novels, animals have magical powers.

The best fantasy novels often:

- Take place in elaborate and magical settings, in completely imaginary worlds.

- Involve talking animals and **mythical** creatures. Such characters can have totally different powers and skills to ordinary human characters.

- Involve lots of magic. Look out for wizards, witches, fairies, goblins and many other fantastic magical beings.

- Have a gripping **plot**, with the brave heroes or heroines fighting against evil.

Science fiction

Science fiction is similar to fantasy in many ways. Both types of novel imagine worlds that don't exist, but science fiction uses science as a starting point. Events in a science fiction novel may be possible at some point in the future, while fantasy worlds will never exist. Some science fiction novels are based on popular science fiction films, such as *Star Wars*, or television series, such as *Doctor Who*.

Science fiction stories often take place on other planets.

Famous fiction

Stephen Hawking is a famous scientist who is well known for his discoveries. He has also written three children's books with his daughter, Lucy Hawking. In the books a character called George goes on adventures across the universe, exploring black holes, investigating alien life and fighting evil scientists.

Stephen Hawking has often written about the science of the universe.

Science fiction novels usually have the following things in common:

- The writer gives a scientific explanation for what happens in the **plot**.

- The story can take the reader away from his or her own life and world.

- The stories are often set far in the future.

- The novels often include amazing inventions and discoveries, and may involve travelling through time.

Mystery stories

Many people enjoy mystery or detective stories. In these novels, the main characters have a problem to solve. This could be a mystery that needs unravelling or a crime that needs to be solved. People enjoy reading mystery stories because they like the puzzle of trying to work out what will happen.

Famous fiction

Some classic mystery stories include Enid Blyton's *Famous Five* series, *Emil and the Detectives* by Erich Kästner, and *The Hardy Boys* and *Nancy Drew* stories. More recently, Lauren St John has written the *Laura Marlin Mysteries* and many readers also enjoy Lauren Child's *Ruby Redfort* books and John Grisham's series featuring mystery-solving teen *Theodore Boone*.

John Grisham is a best-selling author of exciting thrillers for children and adults.

When you read a mystery story, you can look for clues just like the characters!

A good mystery story includes the following things:

- It has unexpected twists that take the reader by surprise. There might also be **red herrings**, which mislead the reader and make them think something else has happened before the truth is revealed.

- The writer slowly reveals clues that the reader can use to work out for him or herself what is happening in the story.

- The stories tend to have very tight **plots**, with the details in every twist and turn making complete sense.

Realistic stories

Some readers like to read stories that are set in the real world. These stories explore what life is like for many people and share true experiences with the reader, rather than taking them away to a made-up world.

Realistic novels have the following features:

- The stories have recognizable settings and characters. The places and people may be in a very different part of the world, but they are based in reality.

- Writers often put their characters in difficult or sad situations. The **plot** often involves the main **protagonists** struggling to overcome these difficulties.

Laura Ingalls Wilder wrote stories based on her own experiences of growing up in the American Midwest.

- The reader really cares about and **empathizes** with the characters in a realistic novel.

- Many realistic novels are set in a different time in history. They might be based on real people and events, or be entirely fictional.

- The writer of a realistic novel needs to take care to include many accurate details to make the world of their story seem real.

Michael Morpurgo has written several books set during the First and Second World Wars.

Write your own

If you want to write a story, it might be easiest to write something realistic. Think about interesting experiences you have had in your life, and the people you know. You could tell a story that will be very different to other people's lives.

Finding the right novel for you

If you already enjoy reading novels, perhaps you could try a **genre** you haven't read before. For example, if you've always read realistic stories, you could try some fantasy or science fiction. Or if you normally stick to books that make you laugh, you could try something different, like a mystery story.

Explore different genres and discover new favourites.

Maybe you are someone who doesn't normally enjoy reading novels. It might be that you haven't found the right book for you yet.

Think about what you enjoy – if you like reading comics and watching comedy shows on television, you might enjoy funny books such as the *Mr Gum* series. If you like non-fiction and finding out facts, you will probably prefer a realistic novel. You could also talk to a librarian or bookseller, or chat to your friends about the books they enjoy.

See for yourself

You could start a book group at your school. Get together with a group of other readers and take it in turns to recommend books to each other. You could lend books to other members of your group or swap stories when you've finished reading them. Encourage each other to try something new!

Take it further...

Do you want to write your own novel? Here are some ways to get started:

1. Always carry a notebook and pen so you can jot down ideas when they pop into your head.

2. Try to read as many books in as many different **genres** as you can.

3. Think carefully about the setting of your story. How can you describe it so the reader really feels what the world in your story is like?

4. Think carefully about your main **protagonist** and all the other characters in your story. Ask yourself lots of questions about each character so you are very clear what they are like.

5. Work out the **plot** of your story. Think about the problems your main character is going to face, and how he or she will overcome them. Who or what will get in his or her way? Can you think of a twist at the end of the story?

6. Keep editing your story until you are happy with it.

Ideas to get you started

Your main character's dog has disappeared. The newspaper is reporting that pets are vanishing all over town. Can your hero follow the clues and solve the mystery of the missing animals?

Your spacecraft has just landed on a faraway planet. You are stepping out on to the planet's surface looking for signs of life. Suddenly you hear a loud explosion...

Your main character's best friend at school has started bullying other kids. What has made the friend change his or her behaviour? Will your main character be able to stop him or her, or will they be bullied too?

Glossary

blurb text on the back cover of a book that briefly describes what the book is about

empathize understand someone else's feelings

fiction story that has been made up

first person when the narrator of a story talks about "I" or "we"

genre particular style of writing

mythical found in myths

narrative account of events in a story

past tense writing that describes events that have already happened

plot storyline

present tense writing that describes events that are happening now

prose writing that is not poetry

protagonist main character

pun joke that uses words with more than one meaning

red herring information that is supposed to mislead the reader

third person when the narrator of a story talks about "her", "him" or "they"

Find out more

Books

Diary of a Wimpy Kid: *Do-It-Yourself Book*, Jeff Kinney (Puffin, 2011)

Get Writing!, Paul Johnson (A&C Black, 2008)

How to Write Stories, Celia Warren (QED, 2008)

Write Your Own Story Book, Louie Stowell (Usborne, 2011)

Websites

www.theguardian.com/childrens-books-site
Read other children's recommendations for novels on this brilliant website all about books.

www.booktrust.org.uk/books/children
The Book Trust website is great for helping you to find novels in different genres for your age.

www.lovereading4kids.co.uk
Search for more recommended novels here.

www.timeforkids.com/homework-helper/writing-tips
There are some excellent writing tips on this website.

Index